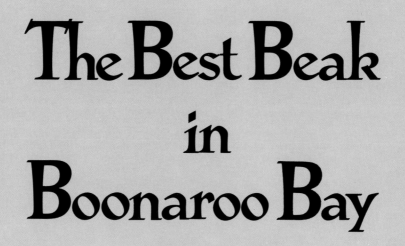

The Best Beak in Boonaroo Bay

Narelle Oliver

fulcrum kids

On most days Boonaroo Bay is a calm and quiet place.

But this was not always so.

One morning, not so very long ago, the birds began to bicker.

And it wasn't a little scuffle over food or nesting places. They were quarrelling about something much more serious: who has the best beak in Boonaroo Bay?

'My beak has the most exquisite shape!' declared the royal spoonbill.

'Exquisite?' scoffed the darter. 'I can't imagine how you catch anything with that monstrosity.'

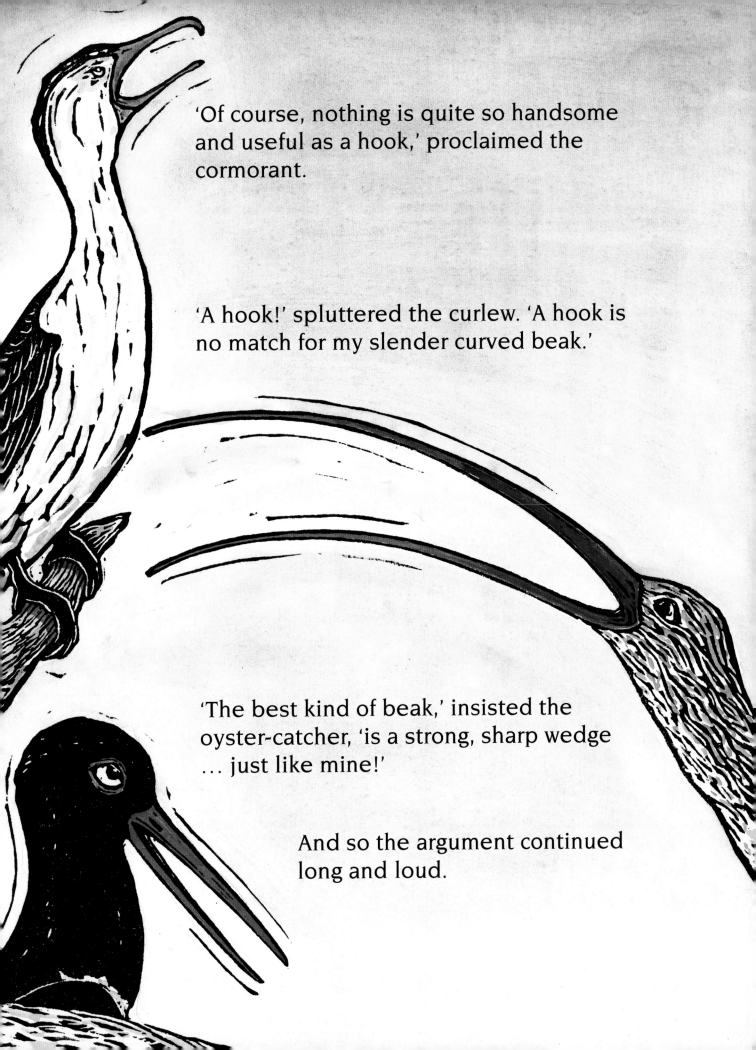

'Of course, nothing is quite so handsome and useful as a hook,' proclaimed the cormorant.

'A hook!' spluttered the curlew. 'A hook is no match for my slender curved beak.'

'The best kind of beak,' insisted the oyster-catcher, 'is a strong, sharp wedge … just like mine!'

And so the argument continued long and loud.

Finally, the wise old pelican spoke:
'If you must decide who has the best
beak in Boonaroo Bay, a contest is
the answer.'

The birds were most impressed with
this idea, and so they began to plan.

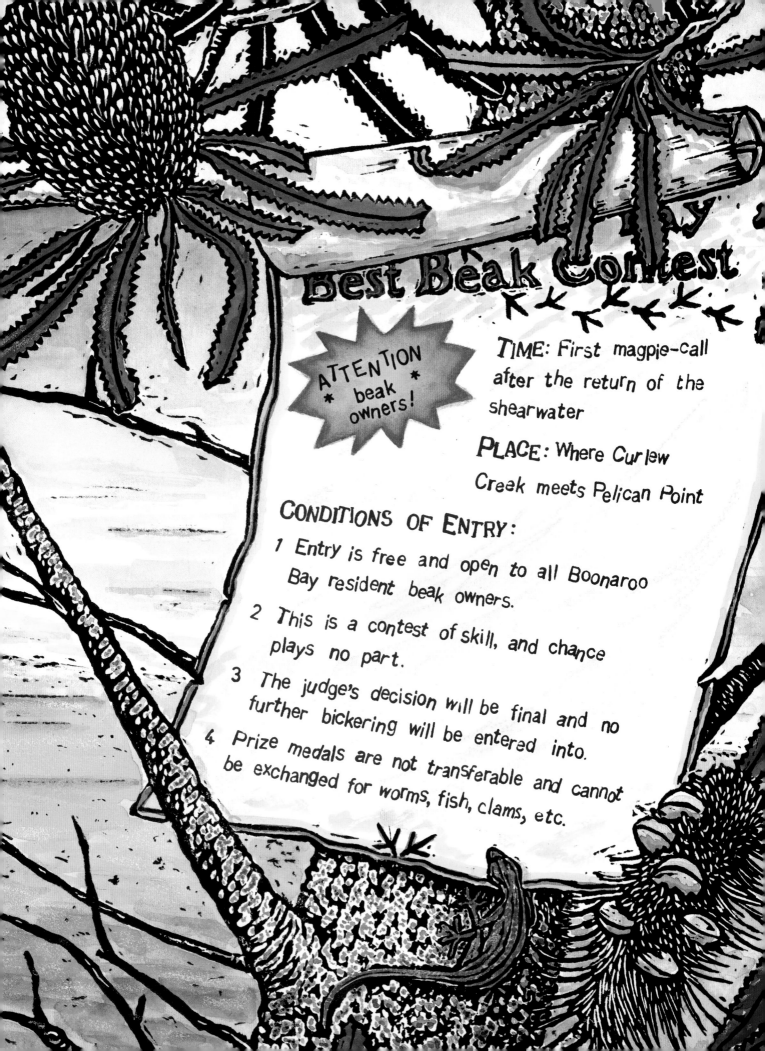

Best Beak Contest

ATTENTION * beak owners! *

TIME: First magpie-call after the return of the shearwater

PLACE: Where Curlew Creek meets Pelican Point

CONDITIONS OF ENTRY:

1 Entry is free and open to all Boonaroo Bay resident beak owners.

2 This is a contest of skill, and chance plays no part.

3 The judge's decision will be final and no further bickering will be entered into.

4 Prize medals are not transferable and cannot be exchanged for worms, fish, clams, etc.

In the twinkling of a sandpiper's eye it was time for the contest to proceed.

'There are five events,' announced the pelican. 'The bird who wins most of these events will have, without a feather of a doubt, the best beak in Boonaroo Bay.'

'Easy,' muttered the spoonbill.

'Let us begin,' continued the pelican. 'To win the first event you must collect the shrimp from the shallow mud near the mangroves.'

Cedarue Bay
Best Beak Contest

Judge

With his wide beak swishing from side to side, the royal spoonbill sieved the mud quickly and thoroughly. In no time he had gathered a pile of shrimp … while the other birds had none.

'I knew my beak was the best!' squawked the spoonbill.

'The contest is not finished yet,' interrupted the pelican. 'To win the next event the contestant must spear a fish!'

Before the others had even flinched a feather, the darter disappeared …

… and then emerged.

'Superbly spiked!' cried the pelican.
'However, the contest is still not over.
To win the next event you must extract a
clam from its rock-hard shell.'

The birds began to hammer and prod.

Except for the oystercatcher.

Carefully, she forced her strong chisel beak between the two parts of the shell and … snap!

'Expertly opened!' exclaimed the pelican.

'But, of course, two events still remain. The winner of the next event must find a worm deep down in the sand.'

This time only the curlew knew what
to do.

'A perfect plunge!' remarked the pelican.

'Now, for the last event you must catch a
slippery, slithery eel.'

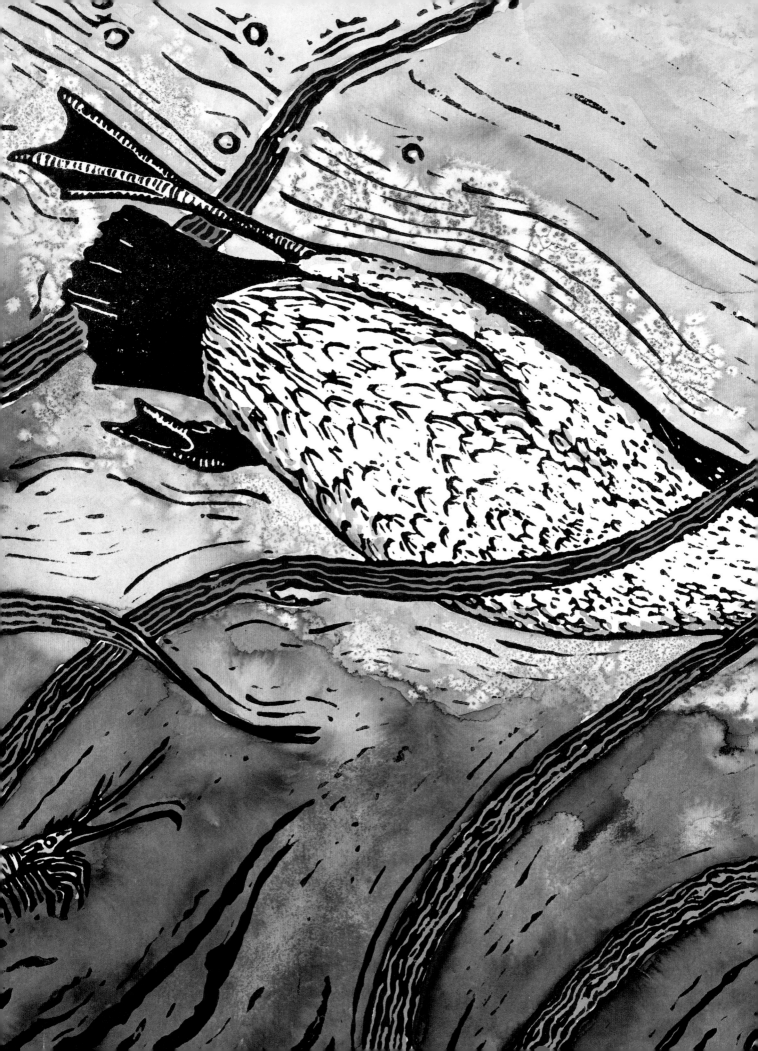

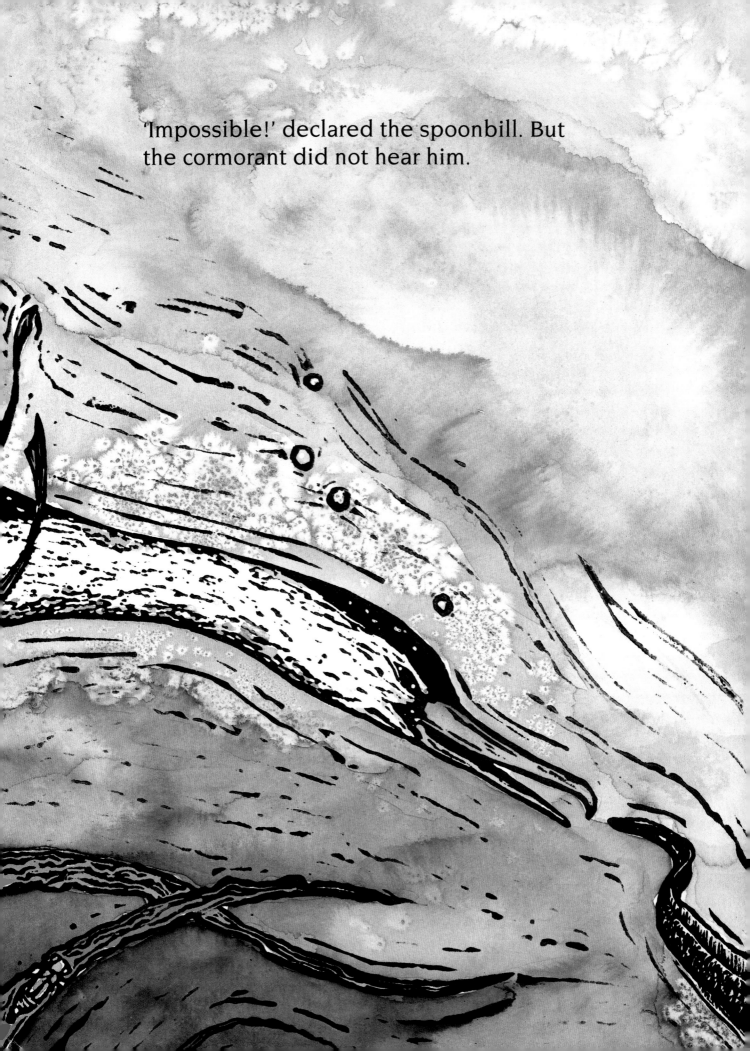

'Impossible!' declared the spoonbill. But the cormorant did not hear him.

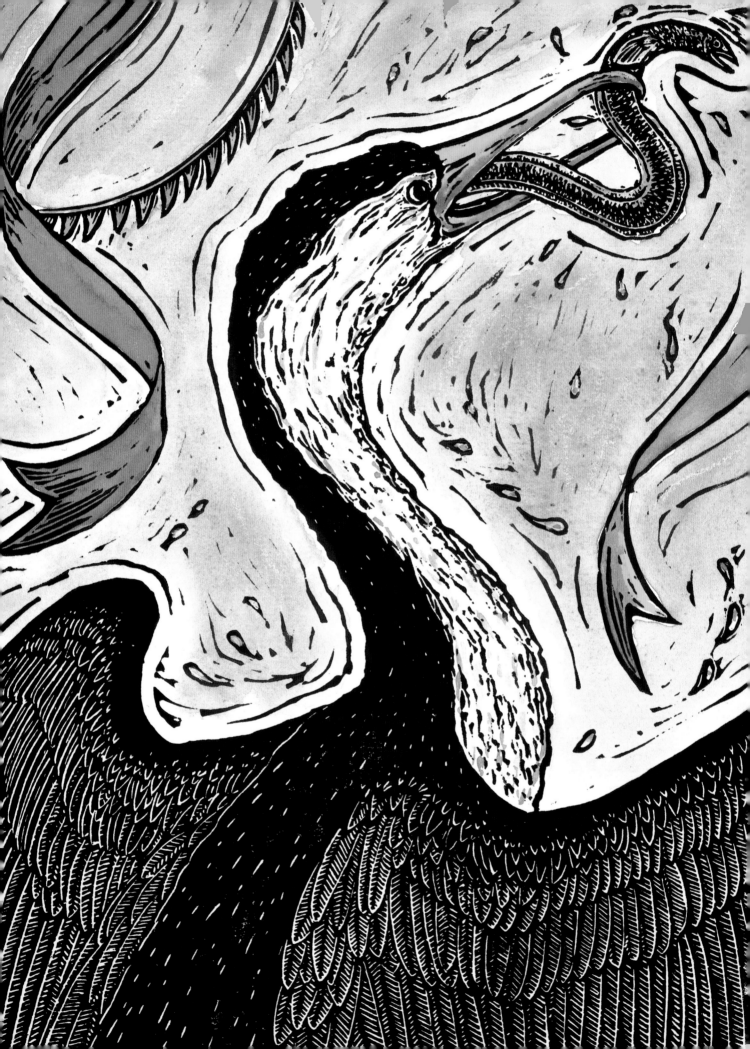

'Magnificently hooked!' shouted the pelican.

'And congratulations to you all.'

'This can't be!' spluttered the spoonbill.

'I'm afraid so,' replied the darter. 'It seems incredible but … it appears that we are all winners. And, indeed, there is no very best beak in Boonaroo Bay.'

Now, there is no need for bickering in Boonaroo Bay. Once again, it is a calm and quiet place.

Except for a splash here and a snap there, as each beak hunts in its own best way.

For Liam

Library of Congress Cataloging-in-Publication Data

Oliver, Narelle.
    The best beak in Boonaroo Bay / Narelle Oliver.
       p.   cm.
    Summary: The birds of Australia's Boonaroo Bay hold a contest to
determine which of them has the best beak.
    ISBN 1-55591-227-3
    [1. Birds—Fiction. 2. Contests—Fiction. 3. Ecology—Fiction.
4. Australia—Fiction.] I. Title.
PZ7.04928f 1995
[Fic]—dc20   95-8075
                                                                                       CIP
                                                                                       AC

Typeset in Novarese by EMS Typesetting
Printed in Korea by Sung In Printing, Inc.

0 9 8 7 6 5 4 3 2 1

Fulcrum Publishing
350 Indiana Street, Suite 350
Golden, Colorado 80401-5093
(800) 992-2908